CHRISTMAS BUSINESS

A TWISTED CHRISTMAS SHORT STORY

ALEXANDRIA BLAELOCK

BlueMere Books
MELBOURNE, AUSTRALIA

For permission requests, please contact
enquiries@bluemerebooks.com.

Ordering Information:
Discounts are available on quantity purchases. For details,
contact orders@bluemerebooks.com.

Christmas Business/Alexandria Blaelock
paperback ISBN: 978-1-925749-97-7
digital ISBN: 978-1-925749-98-4

CHRISTMAS BUSINESS

I had the most disturbing dream.

Or maybe it was a memory...

I was in a scuffed meeting room with pale blue walls, and a grey carpet lit by the steady glow of a fluorescent tube in a reflective holder directly above me.

A plump Caucasian woman wearing a plain navy-blue suit with a white and blue striped button-down shirt sat in the kind of blue plastic stackable chair common in the school rooms I grew up in.

The kind with the nice comfortable curve that hugs your butt, no matter how big it was.

Which was lucky for her.

Her identification card hung on a bright blue lanyard around her neck, but the glare of the light prevented me from reading it.

She sat directly across the scarred "beech" laminated office table from me, her head tilted back, looking up at the polystyrene soundproofing tiles on the ceiling.

Her blonde hair was pulled back in a long ponytail, with a curled fringe like Sandy Olssen's in *Grease*. Upon whom it looked charming, but not so much for the woman.

There was some kind of Christmas song I vaguely recognised piped into the room, and she was humming along.

I was slouched in another blue plastic chair, wondering whether to tell her that her green apple scented body wash was too distinctive.

People would notice it, and therefore her.

Because she was my friend.

But, I knew she'd counter with the idea they would check her out as the source of the aroma, and promptly dismiss her.

Two half-empty white plastic cups of lukewarm dispenser water sat on the table between us.

Through a window on one side, I could see an office with a half-arsed attempt at strings of Christmas decorations, but no people.

And through a screened window on the other, nothing but the hint of sunshine from outside.

I felt drowsy in the mysterious warmth of the room, though I knew I was on the sunny side of the building. I don't know how I knew that, but the knowledge sat in my mind like a stone.

My eyes were shut, so I couldn't see what I was wearing, but I'm fairly sure it was the same as the blonde woman.

The door opened, as did my eyes, and I saw two men walk in. One was a tall, thin, older Caucasian with greying hair.

The other was shorter and by comparison fatter. Intriguingly dark; I had the idea he was Nigerian or Sudanese or something, not American.

They were also wearing navy-blue suits.
I had the idea it was some kind of uniform.

The black guy stood to the side, and a little behind the woman I faced, and the other behind me.

"Thank God," she said sitting up, "I'm so tired of pretending to be her friend."

I tried to stand up to protest, but couldn't move.

The white guy put his hand on my shoulder in case I managed to move, which made me struggle harder, but no matter how hard I strained my muscles, I couldn't move.

"This won't take long," he said, "just a couple of shots."

And then something thin and sharp like a needle hit me in the back of my head and pain blossomed.

I was thinking; this is it; *I'm going to die. They're going to find my splayed body in a filthy alleyway somewhere dressed in some kind of weird Harajuku outfit minus my underpants.*

Because what better way to disguise the death of a mole or a whistle-blower, or whatever I was than as a sex crime.

And with the feel of the second needle in my head, I was gone.

I woke suddenly, bolting upright to touch the back of my head, even before I'd wiped the drool from my mouth or the sleep from my eyes.

Of course there was nothing to feel.

It was just an incredibly vivid dream.

Wasn't it?

"Chasing rabbits in your sleep again Vee?"

I looked towards the male owner of the voice. Noting I was in a pod of four desks. Each person sat with their backs to the others, facing a bright blue partition wall just tall enough to shield us from people walking by.

Thanks to the size and scope of the lavish Christmas decorations strung across the ceiling above me, the hard-wearing, blue-grey geometrically patterned carpet, and the quiet hum of conversation and air-conditioning around me, I could tell we were in an office of some sort.

Though I had no idea where that was.

And, I had no idea who he was, though I was infinitely reassured by his casual outfit of jeans and sloganed t-shirt.

I guessed Vee meant me.

Valerie? Veronica? Vivienne?

I ran out of ideas at that point - the names just felt wrong.

I kept my face perfectly still, trying to not betray my confusion.

"You know, twitching and yelping?"

Had I had this dream before?

Did I make a habit of sleeping at my desk?

I wiped my mouth, then rubbed my eyes.

"Urrrggggghhh," I said.

"You've got to stop working half the night. Go home and get some proper sleep. Come back tomorrow when you're feeling fresher."

Sounded like a great idea, but there was one small hitch.

I didn't know where I lived.

My mouth started watering with that weird metallic taste.

"I'm going to be sick," I said.

He leapt to his feet and rushed me out a door I hadn't noticed and into the male toilets.

Past the urinals where some guy tried to protect his privacy and through to the cubicles.

I would have laughed if I hadn't had my teeth clenched shut, and my hands covering my mouth in case I didn't make it.

He slammed a cubicle door open as my stomach heaved and emptied of what looked like noodles.

Or maybe tapeworms.

Urk.

When it was over, he supported me back to the sinks, where I didn't recognise myself in the mirror.

Not like when you look like shit, but like when you meet someone you have never met before.

Stealing glances at myself, I rinsed my mouth, and splashed water on my face, scrubbing it with my hands, but I still didn't recognise the woman in the mirror.

Weird.

And unsettling.

In the last five minutes he'd been good to me, seeming to know and trust me, so I gambled I could trust him.

"I don't remember who I am," I said, watching his face in the mirror.

He met my eyes, and obviously saw something, because he didn't question my assertion, just put a reassuring hand on my shoulder.

"We need to get you to a hospital straight away."

«« • »»

He came with me, and I wondered if he was my husband. But I wasn't wearing rings.

Boyfriend maybe?

Best friend?

Boss?

Or just a concerned colleague doing the right thing.

While we waited, I checked the handbag he'd given me, starting with the purse.

According to my driver's licence, my name was Vada Paloma and I lived at 2A/22 Smith Street.

It sounded like a made-up name if ever there was one.

My business card told me I worked at Johnstone Industrial Consulting where I was a "consultant."

Whatever that was.

One credit card, one myki, one library and one Medicare card in my wallet along with one $50 note, two $20s, 2 $10s and a $5 neatly stacked facing the same way by order of value, lowest to highest.

No coins, receipts or other ephemera.

An A6 diary told me nothing because when I fanned the pages, there was nothing in it.

Well, not nothing exactly, tucked inside the clear front cover protector was a photo of me, the guy and two others, grinning and holding half-empty pint mugs toward the camera.

"Team Christmas dinner last year," the guy said, then pointed at each of the people said, "Jennifer, Vada, Carl, and me. I'm Jed, your Team Leader." He nudged me with his shoulder, "and best friend."

"How long have I known you?"

"Ah, let's see. You started working here in about October last year."

"That's pretty quick work."

There was something not right about that, but I didn't know what it was.

Even though I was feeling a warm regard for him, I couldn't tell whether that was from his recent care or some memory coming through.

"Yeah, I guess," he said, "but you are everything I didn't know I needed."

Definitely not right. Was I the kind of person who would target him for some reason? Was it something to do that memory/dream?

I turned my attention to the Hello Kitty pen in the diary cover's pen holder.

It was a little worn in the kind of way that suggested I'd used it a lot and had replaced the ink cartridge at least once.

I held it incredulously in front of me - I couldn't believe I was a fan, but the guy... Jed, laughed.

"Secret Santa, from me."

Explained that then.

A set of earbuds, but no phone.

"Where's my phone?" I asked.

"Ah, we check them in each day because we're working on confidential data. We didn't stop at the security desk to pick them up."

And that was the one thing so far that made perfect sense - no company wants their secrets made public, and I was a little bit glad that something made sense.

One key on a generic plastic keyring, so it seemed I didn't have a car.

Sunglasses, umbrella, small Japanese style hand towel, tissues, antiseptic hand wipes, tinted lip balm. And that was it.

Apparently, I travelled light and regularly cleaned out my handbag.

Nothing that told me anything about who I was, aside from someone who wanted to be prepared for eventualities. And that was not suspicious at all...

I felt made up, like a bit character in some spy story with no background.

Jed stayed with me during endless rounds of tests and scans, and during the long hours while I waited for someone to see me.

The short answer was that basically, there was nothing medically wrong. Nothing to suggest *any* kind of brain trauma.

Every single neural and blood test smack dab in the middle of the normal range. The doctor on duty suggested I stop stressing about it, but didn't offer any concrete suggestions about how to do that, or recover my memories.

Unbelievable!

Didn't even keep me in overnight for observation.

Sent the bill to Medicare, and me out onto the street in the wee small hours.

"Can I take you home?" Jed asked.

The truth was I was terrified; both of having lost my memory and going home.

I was not at all sure I wanted him to see anything in my apartment that might reveal who I was, or me trying to make sense of it.

But what if something happened on the way?

And if he was my best friend, wouldn't he have already seen it?

I nodded.

《《 • 》》

My apartment was one of two on the second floor of a three-story building.

He took the key from my hand and unlocked the door for me. Something he did with an easy familiarity, as if taking me home was something he did frequently.

I walked in and looked around me. It was basically two halves, one a "public" space with combined kitchen, dining and lounge, and the other split into a bedroom and combined bathroom and laundry, each with a door through to the other room and each other.

It had all the kind of furniture you'd expect, but there were no signs of me in it.

No art, no personalisation, no mess.

"This looks like a hotel, where's my stuff?"

"It is a hotel. You said you came from interstate and weren't planning to bring your stuff over until you found a place."

I did not point out how full of holes that story was.

"You left your stuff at your place and let it out."

Okay, that was a little more plausible, but for fourteen months?

Who does that?

My doubt must have shown on my face, and he said, "you weren't sure you were going to stay, and things got away from you."

Now that did resonate, so perhaps there was a kernel of truth in there.

I couldn't help myself, I yawned.

"Look, it's been a big day, why don't you get some rest. Don't worry about work, just come in when you feel up to it."

I nodded.

He walked across the room and enveloped me in a hug, "you're going to be okay."

I allowed myself to feel comforted, but I was still afraid.

"Do you want me to stay?"

Yes! Yes please, I thought, but I said, "no, I'm sure I'll be okay."

He kissed my forehead, and I wondered about the strength of our relationship.

Whether we were a thing, or he was taking advantage of the situation.

Or maybe he was holding back.

"No need to follow me out," he said and left.

I walked to the window overlooking the street and watched him walk up to the tram stop.

He turned to wave at me, and I waved back, before getting undressed and falling into the bed.

《《 • 》》

The next morning, I woke early, mainly because I hadn't closed the curtains.

I got out of bed to shut them in the hope of going back to sleep, but once I'd gone room to room, I wasn't really sleepy anymore.

Nonetheless, I lay in bed, looking up at the white ceiling, thinking about the situation I had found myself in.

Common sense had returned during the night. There was no way I'd been injected with something to block my memory by blue-suited people.

That was the stuff of spy thrillers and science fiction, not real life.

I'd just been working too hard, and stressing too much about whatever project I was working on.

The sooner I got back to normal, the better.

So I got up, got dressed, and went to work.

After checking out how to get there.

I clocked Mitchell straight away, perhaps because he was so out of place in the queue to look in the Myer Christmas window amongst all the mothers and hyperactive children.

Too still, and too alone in his navy-blue suit.

I was walking to the office with takeout coffees for the team in the hope they would go easy on me as I recovered my memory.

I was focusing on not spilling them into the cardboard carrier or burning my hands, so I was half a block away before I realised he was the white guy from my dream, and half a block further before I dredged up his name.

A chill ran down my spine as I realised I was looking in the shop windows around me to see if he was following me.

And before I knew what I was doing, I'd cut through an alley and was backtracking my path to lose him.

It seemed I had done this before, so many times I didn't even need to think about it. From deep inside me came a voice that told me he was such a bloody amateur.

I was shaking by the time I got to work.

I sat at my desk, looking at my blank screen thinking through the implications.

There were two options:

1. I worked for or with the navy suits.

2. I had nothing to do with them.

Either way, it seemed the brain injections were intended to delete some or all of my memory.

Because I was undercover at Johnstone's, or because I'd quit working for the navy suits.

Whoever they were.

I asked my gut about the security acronyms; AFP, ABF, ACIC and AUSTRAC didn't ring any bells, neither did ASD, ACSC, ASIO or ASIS. Or even ADF, DIO, and DOD.

None of them felt right.

Which led me back to private industry. And for some reason, that felt worse.

It was all very confusing.

I didn't feel I could confide in Jed, or anyone else for that matter, because who would believe you if you said *I had a dream some guy was doing something awful to me, and then I saw him on the street and now I'm very afraid he and I are up to no good.*

But whether I was a willing participant or not, he'd definitely done something to me.

And then I thought about the blonde woman, she'd said she was tired of pretending to be my friend, and that suggested that whatever it was they were playing at...

We were playing...

Whatever it was they were playing at, it was directed at something nefarious.

So, had she befriended me before or after I arrived at Johnstone's?

Had she lured me to their offices under false pretences, and permitted them to do whatever it was to an innocentish bystander.

Had I been placed at Johnstone's or was I a legitimate employee?

I needed to know more.

I thought the easiest thing would be to investigate myself first.

So, I started with an internet search of my name, and there was absolutely nothing there. Didn't matter which search engine I used, there was nothing to see.

Now it *is* possible I valued my privacy.

And it is equally possible I was planning a career in politics, or a branch of the secret service, and therefore had no social media presence on any of the main channels.

Or that I didn't have any friends.

Or was in a witness protection program.

But it's also possible I was a Luddite.

Bearing in mind I was seemingly the kind of person who was content to leave all her worldly belongings somewhere else for fourteen months.

My driver's license recorded the hotel address, and had a good long expiry, suggesting I had transferred from another state. Or had only just got it.

There was nothing unusual about the license, but if I wanted to access my records, I'd have to fill out a form and send it with a fee I thought was extortionate to their records office.

The Medicare card also had a long expiry, and while I could access my records, I'd need to register and blah blah blah, it sounded like a convoluted process.

The library card had no information, but I supposed they would have records of my loans for however long I'd been a member. Though of course, I couldn't remember my password.

I even checked the drive of the computer I was using, but there were no personal files, and when I questioned that, Jennifer said personal files weren't permitted.

Which I kind of understood, and approved of, because we were dealing with confidential matters.

But which also meant I couldn't keep any notes about myself in the drive as it would be too risky.

Somehow, I got through the day.

I hurried "home" as fast as the peak hour traffic would allow. But on the way, as I sat in the tram, I could smell green apple.

The scent had faded during the day, but it was still detectable.

I looked up and around, partly to check where I was, and partly to check for that bitch Fiona.

If looks could kill...

Well, suffice it to say she'd be raspberry jam lining the tram walls.

However, it seemed that inner me was still cross with her about the "pretending to be her friend" crack.

And I was a little bit impressed with how coolly I saw through her, face impassive, watching her from the corner of my eye, managing not to make eye contact.

So, was she following me, or did she coincidentally live in the area?

She was behind me as I jumped off the tram, so I ducked into a newsagent and bought a notebook.

There was no sign of her when I got back out, but I saw her again as I neared the hotel.

I started to get a little concerned - did we live in the same building? How the hell was I going to manage that?

Once inside my apartment, I opened the windows and saw her lurking in the street.

Which raised a conundrum of sorts. Was I back to being her pretend friend?

I decided to wait for the time being, to see whether she approached me. If we were back together, it shouldn't take long for her to arrive.

I shook myself and poured a glass of wine, grateful I was the kind of person who kept a couple of bottles of wine in my house.

And then, using the memories of every spy movie I could remember seeing, I checked out the apartment; rummaging through all the cupboards and drawers, pulling them out from the walls and looking underneath them.

No unexplainable electronic devices. I didn't actually know what bugs would look like, but I took comfort that the inner me didn't raise any concerns about what she saw.

A small capsule of quality casual clothing. No navy suits.

A couple of fantasy books from the library.

A collection of takeout menus stacked in a rack in the kitchen.

Enough crockery and cutlery for two people, courtesy of the hotel. With enough basic cookware to cook, though it seemed I didn't do any of that.

The usual toiletries and make-up.

A bowl of coins and a couple of hundred in $50 notes, and $30 in $5.

I did not find any records of my previous life, or the current one for that matter.

No real estate agreements, bank statements, employment contract, nothing.

So weird - how could I not have a paper trail?

Nor was there a laptop, or tablet. Though maybe they'd been stolen and I just didn't know it.

There was just me and my phone.

I grabbed out my new notebook and Hello Kitty pen, and sat at the table, but paused, pen wavering over the paper.

Was the reason there was nothing personal in here because I knew I was being monitored?

Did I have a separate room, or maybe another apartment for my personal things?

I put the pen down and closed the book.

I turned the TV on for some noise, and as it was nearly news time, swapped to the couch, settling down with the phone.

«« • »»

I woke up on the floor with a blinding headache. I opened one eye and looked around me; it was dusk. I started freaking out thinking it was tomorrow.

Then patted the floor around me to find my phone and checked the time, which was difficult because I couldn't see properly.

I thought the wiggly, staticky, blurry numbers indicated the same day, about an hour later.

I relaxed a little.

For the lack of being able to think of any better way to ease the pain at that moment, I crawled across the floor to the bathroom, stood wobbling as I drank some water, splashed my face and rinsed a flannel in water as hot as I could take it, then dropped back down on the floor and lay with it on my forehead.

After a while, the flannel cooled, and I turned it over just in case the other side was warmer.

And a little after that, I managed to lever myself upright and stagger to the kitchen.

I was cold, so I pulled the blanket off the bed on my way through.

The TV was still on, seeming especially bright, and if it was trying to remind me of something.

Mesmerised, I dropped to the couch, pulled the blanket more tightly around my shoulders, and looked at it.

I wasn't watching the TV per se, but I could see/remember flashes that weren't there before.

Wearing a low-cut slinky dress, dancing with strangers.

Glimpses of navy suited people; not the ones in my first dream memory but others.

Some gorgeous boy who I knew, but couldn't remember.

I couldn't tell whether the new memories were this life or the one before.

Then I heard a Christmas song on the TV, over an ad for some kind of sale.

And it clicked into place.

Not my memory, unfortunately, but that some kind of Christmas song had triggered new/old memories.

Deductively, the song that had been playing that day with the needles.

Presumably, I'd heard it the day before when I'd forgotten who I was.

And probably again on the TV just then when I blacked out.

So, I'd answered one question I didn't know I had, and triggered a billion more.

Had I been conditioned, or was it coincidental?

If I'd been conditioned, was I supposed to lay low for a year? Had they chosen a Christmas song so I wouldn't be triggered until now?

Were the navy suits hanging around waiting for my memory to come back?

Circling back through to were they "good" people or not?

And whether I should call Jed.

And almost immediately back to not really having anyone I could trust or rely on, except myself.

So, what was the trigger, and could I hear it without losing consciousness?

The TV was one of the ones that record a buffer, so you can pause, rewind, and fast forward.

Go to the toilet anytime you wanted, not cross your legs and wait for an ad break.

I rewound it to about where I remembered it being, and then punched the play button.
And set my phone to record it too.

I skimmed through the game shows, then played the ads, and about 15 minutes later I saw the one.

I started to feel ill with heartburn and nausea. I couldn't seem to get enough air in my lungs.

Time seemed to slow down, and every syllable stabbed me in the head.

I felt dizzy.

So very tired.

I lay on the floor gasping, trying to find the remote to turn the TV off with my useless fingers that seemed to have grown to an enormous size.

But the worst thing of all, was that I didn't recognise the song.

Then I was floating in another sea of blackness

《《 • 》》

This time, I woke in a hospital, feeling thirsty and hungover.

But fortunately, a room to myself.

I was pretty sure it wasn't the same hospital Jed had taken me to before.

But it had the same kind of lino on the floor with the edges that curved a little way up the wall to form a seamless skirting board.

And the same kind of textured tiles on the ceiling, presumably to dampen the sound of moaning from the next room. And if that was the case, it wasn't what you might call effective.

In my case, there was a stain on the tiles right above my bed that looked a bit like a cherub if you narrowed your eyes and looked at it like one of those 3D puzzle drawings.

And of course, the smell of boiled cabbage and processed meat flavoured bread crumbs for dinner.

A plastic jug of water, along with a plastic glass with a straw in it sat on a rolling table that had been pushed to the side.

And beyond the water jug, through the window, treetops and the kind of glow you get from street lights, or those bright lights over sports grounds.

No way the gauge when I was.

Something heavy weighed on my hand, and when I looked, it was someone else's hand and their head as well.

It looked a bit like Jed.

I twitched, and he jolted awake, "what's going on?" he said.

I gave him a minute, and then he asked, "what's the time?"

"I could ask you the same, but I'll ask for water first."

He grunted as he stood up and staggered to the table to drag it over. Then poured some water into the glass and held it a little under my chin where I could reach the straw.

And filled it up three times until I wasn't thirsty anymore.

"Other end?" he asked.

And I realised I needed to pee.

He helped me up and out of the bed, holding the rickety drip pole, escorting me through the bathroom door.

"Need any help with..." he gestured at me, then the toilet, in an embarrassed kind of way.

For a moment I was tempted to say yes, just to see how he'd handle that, but I said no.

"I'll be just outside, so let me know when you're ready."

I sat there for a while, wondering how I'd got to the hospital.

Someone must have come in, but who, and how.

I cleaned myself up, then called out, "I'm on my way."

He opened the door and stepped in to pick up the drip pole and take me back to the bed.

He plumped up the pillows before helping me back in.

And after all that, I was exhausted.

"So, what is the time after all that," I asked.

"Around three am. Do you need anything?"

I thought about it for a little. A cup of tea was tempting, but I was more tired than desperate for tea, so I said no.

"Go back to sleep then," he said, "I'll be here when you wake up."

And even though I had questions circling my brain, I did just go back to sleep.

《《 • 》》

The next morning I was woken by one of those ruthlessly efficient nurses, and Jed was nowhere to be seen.

"Where's my friend?" I asked.

"What friend," she said, "there's no one here but you."

I wondered if I'd dreamt him, or if he'd really been there.

She took my observations, and that made me wonder why no one had done them before.

Unless I was so very deeply asleep I didn't notice.

Or in a coma.

Or...

I couldn't think why else I might not have noticed.

She bustled away, refusing to answer any questions, only saying "doctor will be here soon."

Someone came in with cold white bread toast and little packets of margarine and strawberry jam for breakfast.

But given I hadn't eaten anything for dinner, I was hungry enough to eat them and very tempted to ask for another serve.

To wash it down, reconstituted orange juice, and a cup of lukewarm water with a teabag, one packet of sugar, and one single-serve pod of preserved milk, unaccountably served refrigerated.

By no means the best breakfast ever.

And then I waited for someone to come.

For Jed, or the doctor, or someone else to relieve the tedium of being in a single room with nothing to read and no phone to stream a show or play a game on.

After about a thousand years, a doctor arrived, clean and fresh with a crisp shirt and tied under his lab coat. Smelling of soap and some kind of woodsy cologne.

I was suddenly conscious of how dishevelled I was.

He seemed familiar, and as he flashed a torch in my eyes, and poked my face, and took my blood pressure, I was trying to place him.

He started humming a Christmas song, and I started to feel ill.

When he smiled at that, I knew who he was - the third guy from that room. The Nigerian or Sudanese or whatever guy.

I tried to scoot up the bed away from him, but he grabbed my shoulders to stop me.

At least he stopped humming.

"How did you find me?"

"We knew at some point you'd wake up to yourself, so we've been monitoring hospital admissions."

That wasn't reassuring in the slightest, "is this your doing?"

He smiled slightly, "it is and it isn't."

"For god's sake, stop dancing around the issue and tell me."

"What do you remember?"

Obviously I wasn't going to *tell* him I remembered nothing; I countered, "are you even a doctor?"

"I am."

He looked closely at me, looking for I don't know what, then sighed.

"My name is Aminu. I work for Jinko Cult Deprogramming."

"Cult Deprogramming? What the..."

"You followed Gregory John James into the Arcane Workers, intending to bring him out, but—"

"The what?"

"The Arcane Workers, does that resonate with you?"

The thing was I had never heard of them, but it felt true, so after a pause, I nodded.

I didn't trust him...

Them...

Whatever, but at least I was getting some answers.

"The Arcane Workers is a self-help type of cult, mainly targeting unemployed people with books and seminars.

"But some are drawn into their intensive, live-in programmes where you're essentially working as slave labour."

A chill went down my spine as I thought about that gorgeous boy I couldn't remember, "I followed him into the live-in programme."

"That's right."

"So what happened to... James, did you say?"

"Ah, he didn't make it," Dr Aminu made a sad face.

"Didn't make it out of the group, or didn't survive?"

"I'm sorry."

I was aghast - how could they get away with something like that, "they *killed* him?"

"Not as such, more along the lines of overworking and underfeeding."

So, they "just" stood by and let him work himself to death. That was criminal enough for me.

"And what are you doing about it?"

"We are sharing the information we've been gathering with the responsible Police Forces."

"I see."

I tried to summon up more memories, something that might be useful, but I was drawing a blank.

Aminu waited, and eventually asked, "do you remember who I am," he asked.

"I remember you being there when whatever that was in my head happened, and if you're a doctor, was that strictly ethical?"

"Intensive acupuncture. We had installed certain blocks prior to sending you in, and were trying to remove them.

"Do you remember who you are?"

"No."

"The name we gave you is Vada Paloma, but the name you were born with is Lily Robertson."

Lily Robertson; I rolled the name around in my head, and it felt right.

I tried to remember Lily's life, and there was nothing much, just the taste of vanilla on my tongue. I shook my head.

"We were unable to remove the blocks, so we left you with the implanted memories we gave you when you infiltrated the Workers. Am I correct that you don't have access to those either?"

By this point, I thought I could probably trust him, so I said "yes."

"And would I be correct in thinking you would like to remember your previous life?"

"Yes."

"It won't be comfortable."

I barely hesitated, "I will stick it out for as long as it takes."

"I know you will. You weren't ready to let it go last time, but I think you might be now."

What followed was two weeks of agony at a luxurious private clinic.

That Christmas song piped into my room non-stop.

Blinding headaches.

Throwing up almost as soon as I'd eaten.

Fitful sleep.

Punctuated by a succession of acupuncture treatments and herbal tonics.

Saunas and massages more like going twenty rounds with a giant kickboxing spider wearing boxing gloves.

Starving, feverish, freezing.

Until I lay on the floor like something you'd wipe off your shoe.

But at least I remembered who I was, and why that level of secrecy was required.

Though I'm still not entirely sure I was one of the good guys.

《《 • 》》

I was lying in a deck chair taking the sun when Jed arrived, drowsy in the warm eucalyptus-scented sunshine.

Magpies warbling from the treetops.

I'm not entirely sure who was more surprised, me or him because I'd been hoping I wouldn't see him again.

I had no idea what to say to him.

After all, I'd lied to him, even if I hadn't been aware of it at the time.

He stood looking at me, which was making me uncomfortable, so I stood up to talk to him.

And it seemed he didn't know what to say either.

"How have you been?" I asked at the same time as he said, "you look different," and we both laughed.

"Let's go for a walk around the gardens," I said, "they're really lovely," thinking I'd need the benefit of the exercise to stimulate my brain.

We walked across the sun deck, down the stairs following the path around a corner, out of sight of the buildings, he asked, "are you okay now?"

"Ummm. If you mean do I have my memory back, then yes, but I'm not sure how I feel about that."

"Vee, I—"

"My name is Lily Robertson, not Vada Paloma."

He didn't say anything for a while, not until we'd walked around a garden bed full of unattractive purple azaleas, "Lily suits you much better."

We walked a little further and I decided to just spit it out.

"I worked for a cult deprogrammer, though as a career choice it holds very little appeal for me now.

"It seems I went a bit too far undercover, and couldn't get back."

We circled some kind of weird geometric sculpture and started returning to the buildings.

He didn't say anything.

"I'm sorry I lied to you."

Still he didn't say anything, so I started resigning myself to starting a third life somewhere else.

As we were about to climb the stairs, he paused and looked at me, searching my face. "I've been trying to imagine it, but I can't. It must have been hard for you," he said.

Which was pretty much the last thing I'd imagined he might say.

"I guess your training helps you to become the person you need to be to achieve your objective, and that I have no idea who you are."

I shrugged, I couldn't deny it. That was exactly what I had done to win him over.

"I wonder whether the "real" you might be a more interesting person."

I did not shrug again, though I wanted to. I just waited to hear what he said next.

"But you were an excellent analyst and Johnstone's is prepared to keep you on, if you're willing."

I scuffed the ground with a toe, "and you?"

"I don't know."

"I don't want to make you uncomfortable, so I will decline if you're unsure."

He looked at me again, and I resisted the temptation to pat the air around my head to see if I'd grown a second head.

"You've been such a big part of my life last year that I just can't imagine you not being there."

I held my breath.

"And I'm so curious about who you are."

His smile caught me by surprise, and I gave him one of mine.

"Shall we give it a try?"

"I'd like that?"

"So, we'll see you on Monday then. Let's say 9 am?"

"I wouldn't miss it for the world."

THE END

ABOUT THE AUTHOR

Alexandria Blaelock writes stories, some of them for *Ellery Queen's Mystery Magazine* and *Pulphouse Fiction Magazine*. She's also written five self-help books applying business techniques to personal matters like getting dressed, cleaning house, and feeding your friends.

As a recovering Project Manager, she's probably too fond of sticking to plan. She lives in a forest because she enjoys birdsong, the scent of gum leaves and the sun on her face. When not telecommuting to parallel universes from her Melbourne based imagination, she watches K-dramas, talks to animals, and drinks Campari. At the same time.

Discover more at www.alexandriablaelock.com.

BOOKS BY
ALEXANDRIA BLAELOCK

SHORT STORY COLLECTIONS

The Histories of Hayward Hall
Lovelorn, Lovestruck and Love at First Sight
Common or Garden Variety Heroes
Case Files of the Wilkinson Detective Agency
Unavoidable Fates
Christmas Travesties

OTHER FICTION

That Love Nonsense

MS BLAELOCK'S BOOKS

Stress Free Dinner Parties
Signature Wardrobe Planning
Holistic Personal Finance
Minimally Viable Housekeeping
Planning a Life Worth Living

SELECTED SHORT STORIES

Alma's Grace
Balancing the Book
Carmelita Basingstoke
Fate in Your Hands
Kiss of Death
Lady of the Looking Glass
Life in the Security Directorate
Long Weekend in the Snow
Love in the Past Tense
Love in the Security Directorate
Morning Star, Evening Star, Superstar
Needy Bitch
Payton's Run
Phoenix Child
Secret Singer
Shining Star
Ship in a Bottle
Simone Says Hands in the Air
Special Relativity in Space
The Bygone Boyfriend
The Day the Schedule Broke
The Ghost Detectors
The Guardian's Vigil
The Mince Pie Mystery
The Mystery of the Master Suite
The Pseudonym's Bride
The Shadow Thieves
The Time-Space Paradox
Toy Soldiers